Scrapbooks of America™

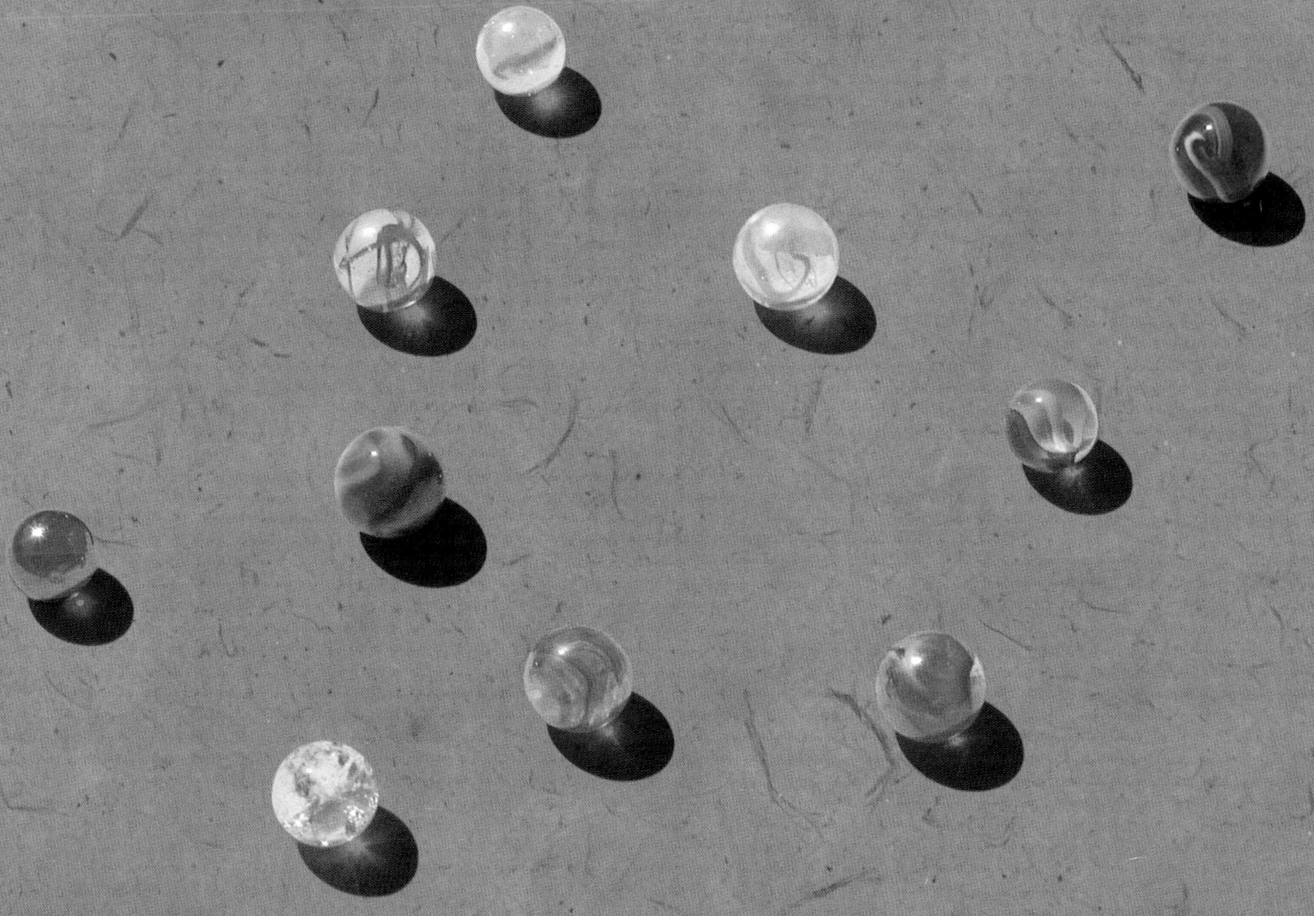

Published by Tradition Books™ and distributed to the school and library market by The Child's World®
P.O. Box 326, Chanhassen, MN 55317-0326 ➝ 800/599-READ ➝ http://www.childsworld.com

An Editorial Directions book
Editors: E. Russell Primm and Lucia Raatma
Additional Writing: Lucia Raatma and Alice Flanagan/Flanagan Publishing Services
Photo Selector: Lucia Raatma
Photo Researcher: Alice Flanagan/Flanagan Publishing Services
Proofreader: Chad Rubel
Design: Kathleen Petelinsek/The Design Lab

Library of Congress Cataloging-in-Publication Data
Dell, Pamela.
  Liam's watch : a strange story of the Great Chicago Fire / by Pamela J. Dell.
    p. cm.
Summary: Twelve-year-old Liam and his family must flee their home when a fire rages through Chicago in 1871.
Includes notes on the Great Chicago Fire and suggests creative writing, scrapbook, and family history activities.
  ISBN 1-59187-014-3 (library bound : alk. paper)
  1. Great Fire, Chicago, Ill., 1871—Juvenile fiction. [1. Great Fire, Chicago, Ill., 1871—Fiction. 2. Fires—Illinois—Chicago—Fiction. 3. Chicago (Ill.)—History—To 1875—Fiction.] I. Title.
  PZ7.D3845 Li 2002
  [Fic]—dc21   2002004654

Scrapbooks of America™

LIAM'S WATCH
A Strange Story of the Great Chicago Fire

By Pamela Dell

TRADITION BOOKS™
EXCELSIOR, MINNESOTA

J

TABLE OF CONTENTS

I couldn't say why my eyes flew open like that, bringing me so abruptly out of sleep. Sometimes it seems as if your mind is wide awake somehow, even while your body is fast asleep. It's almost as if some-times one eye remains closed while the other is wide open, staring into the dark of night. The closed eye looks inward at dreams, **lulling** you, while the open eye moves restlessly back and forth, alert for danger. At least this was how it seemed to me.

I often had a strange sense of things like that. I knew things. I felt them going on unseen, all around me. Things other people couldn't even begin to sense. So even though I wasn't sure what it was that woke me that night, I knew it was something bad.

It wasn't the ghost of my little brother, either, that caused me to wake so suddenly. If it had been him, I wouldn't have been much alarmed, to tell the truth. For wee Brian had been so good in life that I knew he couldn't harm a soul, especially me, even if he were a ghost. Brian died in 1870. Nearly a year and a half before the great disaster that took our city down to ashes. He died of **pneumonia,** and he wasn't even ten years old yet at the time. His sudden passing like that left a hole in the center of our family. A hole I felt I could almost look down into, filled with a strange darkness. So whenever I started to think about

Our parents moved to Chicago from Ireland and felt right at home. The Irish and Germans were the largest groups of immigrants to settle in the city.

6

Before the Great Fire, Chicago was having a heat wave after a long, dry summer.

In October 1871, Chicago was having an Indian Summer. Since July 4, only 1 1/2 inches (3.8 centimeters) of rain had fallen in the city.

Chicago's Field, Leiter & Co. department store, on the corner of State and Washington Streets

him, or to look into that hole, I concentrated on putting my mind on other things.

"Have peace, Liam," Father Cady said to me at Brian's wake. "Brian's fled to heaven. Ye can rest assured he's well taken care of there, lad." I hoped the priest was right. Secretly, though, I felt there was no way truly to be sure of that fact. But I said nothing.

With Brian gone, our bedroom became all mine. I'd wanted my own room before he got sick. Every boy does. But after I got it, it seemed too empty without Brian there, asleep in the next bed. I felt he might be somewhere nearby, drifting in a corner maybe. Perhaps he was watching what I was thinking as I settled into sleep. Imagining such a possibility gave me a strange feeling indeed.

But when my eyes flew open like that, late in the night of October 8, 1871, I didn't sense Brian anywhere around. My room was lit with an **eerie,** reddish glow, like wavering streaks of blood on the walls. A strange grit was in the air.

It had been hot as a coal fire all day. Now with my window wide open, the pale linen curtains were lifting and moving like ghostly sleeves in the night breeze. But there was nothing cooling about this breeze as it blew across my face. Instead it was pure roasted air. It was, in fact, not a breeze at all but a forceful and strange-smelling wind. And tiny, fiery particles seemed to be dropping into my throat with every breath I took.

I sat up in bed and grabbed my pocket

watch from the bedside table. It was made of the finest silver and felt heavy and familiar in my hand. It had belonged to my grandfather, who had lived and died in Dublin, Ireland. Now it belonged to me in Chicago, Illinois. It was my most prized possession.

In the light of the flickering red shadows, I read the time: 11:24. The whole house was asleep. Everyone but me. I moved to get out of bed. O'Toole, who had been sleeping across my feet, raised his head as I stirred. His tail beat happily against the **bedclothes** as I stroked his glossy, golden coat. Then I threw back the covers and padded across the room.

At the window, when I went to part the

10

My grandfather's pocket watch
was a special treasure.

O'Toole was a constant companion in our family.

curtains, the shudder of a **premonition** went through me. It suddenly seemed that I wasn't looking at my own hand at all. Instead, those grasping, eager fingers seemed to have an existence all of their own. It was a **disembodied** hand, completely detached from any body and floating in the night. I watched the hand reach out, as fascinated as if I were watching a magician's trick. Watch now, people! The "disembodied hand" is about to part the curtain! What terrible thing is hiding on the other side?

In that moment, I knew with perfect certainty what the scene would be behind those **ominously** fluttering curtains. Before I even saw it with my eyes, the image of what lay beyond showed itself to my mind, as surely as if I were viewing a detailed painting. I knew I was about to witness the horror that had kept my watching eye open while I had been sleeping.

I waited, as still as a statue in the blood-red tinge of my room. Holding my breath. Not ready yet to take in such a **spectacle** as I knew lay spread out beyond my window.

There had been a bad fire just the night before, Saturday night. It had raged on for seventeen hours and burned down every building on four whole blocks of the city before the firemen were able to stop it.

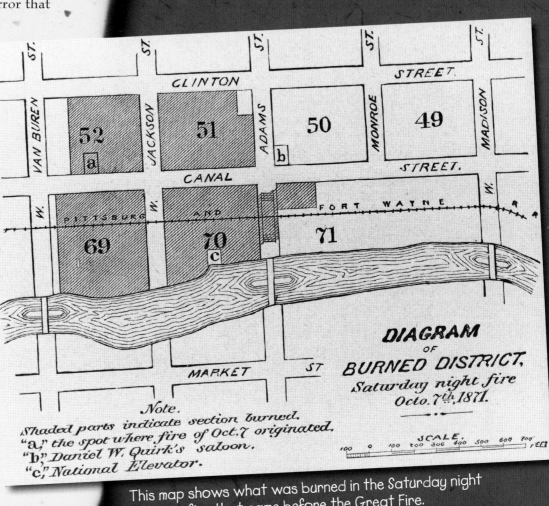

DIAGRAM
OF
BURNED DISTRICT,
Saturday night fire
Octo. 7th 1871.

Note.
Shaded parts indicate section burned.
"a" the spot where fire of Oct. 7 originated.
"b" Daniel W. Quirk's saloon.
"c" National Elevator.

This map shows what was burned in the Saturday night fire that came before the Great Fire.

George Francis Train did more than give public lectures. He developed land in Omaha, Nebraska, and helped build some of the railroads in the western United States.

George Francis Train was a successful businessman who also gave lectures about events of our time.

The strange tale that Papa had told us when he and Mum came home from their Saturday night out came suddenly into my mind.

They had gone to hear a man named George Francis Train give a lecture at Farwell Hall. Mr. Train was so popular that Papa had had to use his best business connections to get two seats to the lecture. My older brothers, Michael and Billy, and I had all waited up for their return to hear about it, too. Even before Papa told us Mr. Train's final words, I'd already felt a kind of **dread.** It seemed to accompany my parents through the door. And then it settled on me. So I wasn't surprised when Papa quoted to us Mr. Train's mysterious prediction.

Papa's voice rose like a battle cry in imitation of Mr. Train.

"This is the last public address that will be delivered within these walls!" Papa shouted, raising a fist and shaking it at the ceiling. His dark eyebrows wrinkled. "A terrible **calamity** is impending over the city of Chicago! More I cannot say! More I dare not utter!"

Then Papa had burst into hearty laughter. My two older brothers found this theatrical outburst equally amusing. Their own laughter rose and mingled with Papa's, filling the parlor. But through the whole thing, Mum sat still and silent, twisting her handkerchief into a knotted strand between her fingers. To look at her you would have thought Mr. Train's strange calamity was about to fall on our very house in the next moment.

But it took another day for that calamity to occur.

I stood a second longer before the window, and then I grabbed the curtain and yanked it back. There beyond the window, just as I had imagined it, was the calamity. There was the vast city, spreading out to the west and to the south before me. But it was not a city covered in darkness as it should have been. Off to the southwest, a huge wall of flame was climbing into the sky. Its wicked fiery arms were reaching in all directions, intent on a smothering destruction, it seemed. Even at a distance, those flames looked huge, raw, and as red-orange as dragon's breath.

The Crosby Opera House was one of the many landmarks that was destroyed by the fire.

This family was trapped on the roof of their house as the city burned.

The fire was a ferocious, seething sea that appeared to be rolling straight toward us, on a line from southwest to northeast. There was a kind of **din,** too, though I wondered if I were only imagining it. But no, I was sure I could hear the sounds, terrible sounds. The roar of fire, the thunder of explosives. I felt sure I could even hear screaming.

I was frozen. And then I was the one who screamed.

"Fire!!"

O'Toole jumped up, and a wild yelp rose from his throat. He sprang to the floor, his toenails clicking on the wooden planks as he followed me to the door. I flung it open and shouted into the hall.

"Fire, Papa! Fire!"

The next second, doors were opening. Our whole house came alive with activity. Mum and Papa, looking weary, came into the hall, wrapping their robes around them. Billy staggered from his room, rubbing his eyes. Michael was already half dressed.

In a moment, we were all gathered at the wide bay window in the upstairs landing. Outside, but a few miles off, the sky was lit by showers of sparks, a vast drapery of fire. For several minutes we stood together in awed silence, watching.

Nobody moved nor said a thing. It came to my thought that they were all **mesmerized** by the beauty and the intensity of what we

Firefighters were already exhausted before the Great Fire began. They had worked all Saturday night putting out another blaze in the city.

were seeing.

"We have to get out!" I screamed, wanting only to rouse them from their **hypnotic** state.

"Calm yourself, Liam, my son," Papa said, turning away and now focusing on me. He put a hand on my shoulder, but his face was serious.

"It's going to burn down the whole house, Papa!" I cried.

"No, no," Papa said in an even voice. "'Tis still far off from here. That fire will

Chicago's industrial area in flames

According to legend, the fire began in the barn of Patrick and Catherine O'Leary on the Near West Side of Chicago. Some say that a cow knocked over a lantern, but that story has never been proven to be true.

The Chicago Courthouse, originally built in the 1850s, as it appeared in the days before the fire

never get so far as this." Then he turned to Mum.

"I best go check on the shop though. I'll take Michael and Billy, as we may need to move and carry some things. I wouldn't want to lose that new shipment of silver."

"I want to go, too!" I said.

McCorkle's Linen, Lace & Silver was one of the finest shops on all of Lake Street. Papa's pride. He had begun to build it up from the day he and Mum arrived from Ireland, newly married. Now it had made him wealthy and important all round the city.

"Och, son!" Papa said to me when I

pleaded again, "you're but a lad of twelve. We won't have ye out in this. No, ye best stay here and watch over your ma."

I wanted to scream out my protests. Insist to be taken along with my brothers. Michael was only five years older than I, and Billy only four. Why should they be allowed and not me? But I held my tongue for fear Mum would be upset. Who would stay with her if I left?

* * *

For the next hour, we waited. Mum made tea for us, but we barely spoke at all. It was just before 1:00 A.M. when there came a **commotion** in the front of the house and Billy shot through the door.

"Come on!" he shouted to us. "Mum! Liam! Papa's sent me back to fetch you. They say the fire is out of control. Everything's burning!"

"Not the fireproof buildings?" Mum asked as we rushed to meet him in the front hall.

"Fireproof?!" Billy scoffed. "One downtown building after another is falling in ashes. It's a terrible scene. They think it'll burn all the way to the lake. We must gather what we can and get away. Now!"

"But surely the store's all right, Billy?" Mum asked. Billy took a deep breath and looked out through the open front door. A fiery backdrop outlined the dark and sleeping houses of our neighborhood.

"Doesn't look good, Mum," he said finally.

Even though the fire seems to have started in their barn, the O'Learys' cottage survived the fire.

Crowds running to safety as the Chamber of Commerce burned

He looked back to her. "Papa and Michael are fine. They're doing the best they can. But Papa fears it'll all be gone. We must pack some things and leave the house right now."

"But where will we go, Billy?" I wanted to know.

"Papa says we should go as fast as we can to Uncle Ryan's. It's supposed to be safe over the river in the western division where he is. They'll meet us there."

"But what if it's burning there, too?" Mum's voice was trembling.

"The winds are fierce, but they're moving toward the lake," Billy said. "I'm going to the coach house to hitch up Bess. Be quick! We haven't got a minute!"

After Billy had gone out back, my feet

The neighborhoods west of the city survived the fire.

Prized marbles were among the possessions we took the time to save.

flew. Upstairs in my room, I packed my most important things in a small leather box. A bag of glass marbles, all colors, and several big cat's eye shooters. The Bible Mum had given me for confirmation. Gold cufflinks and a colorful top that I'd got for my last birthday. Five silver dollars. A photo of wee Brian and me, held in a tin frame. Everything that was precious to me. On top of it all, I placed Gramp's pocket watch, which now read 1:03 A.M.

I closed the lid on the leather box and turned the latch. Downstairs I was surprised to see Mum standing before a small trunk she'd placed on the dining room table. Her hands were inside it as she stared down, unmoving. Billy was behind her now, holding her shoulders as if wanting to pull her away. I knew what was in that trunk: Brian's clothes. She had gathered nothing more.

"Liam!" Billy looked relieved to see me. He nodded his head toward the back of the house.

"Come on, Mum," he said gently. He tightened his grip on her shoulders and pulled her away from the trunk. Though she let out a small cry of protest, she didn't resist. Quickly I snapped the trunk shut, put my box on top of it, and followed them out, carrying both.

As Bess pulled us off down the street and away from home, I hugged O'Toole close to me. He licked my face and I patted his head. Then I looked back. Our house stood solemn and elegant, three stories high. All its windows were tinted red from the fire's terrifying reflection. It looked like a dozen reddish, haunted eyes staring out at coming destruction. I knew in that moment it would be the last I ever saw of our house, and I kept my eyes on it till we rounded a corner and I could see it no more.

All around us now the air was hot and terrible. Sparks flew in the night above our heads in constant showers. We were heading into a snowstorm of **embers.** And the noise was terrible.

We came into the broad expanse of Randolph Street, and it was there that I truly

The Great Chicago Fire burned for 27 hours and destroyed 17,450 buildings.

Once we loaded our belongings into the wagon, our lives changed forever.

felt we'd driven into one of the **thoroughfares** of hell, for it reminded me of pictures I had seen at Sunday School.

People of every level of society were mixed together in panic, screaming, tearing at each other. Fist-fighting and brawling. Horses were leaping in fear, straining at their harnesses. Men and women alike were carrying babies, potted plants, old suitcases, and pets. Some had bolts of fabric or stacks of dishes. A man passed us dragging a crate of books. Everywhere the street was littered with abandoned possessions, making it nearly impossible to move up the street.

As Billy maneuvered our wagon carefully forward, Mum sat beside him, both hands clapped over her mouth and her dark eyes wide with horror. The heat was so intense now I felt my shirt sticking close to my back, completely drenched. The roar of the fire seemed the worst, the most deafening sound I had ever heard.

Off to the left somewhere, a huge explosion ripped the night, and I feared that a nearby building must have collapsed.

"What was that?" I screamed up to Billy.

He shouted back at me over his shoulder. "They're using explosives to blow up buildings in hopes of stopping the fire that way! Hang on, Liam. I'm going to try to get Bess to go a bit faster. I fear all the bridges will be burning before we reach a one of them!"

Approximately three hundred people died in the Great Fire.

Armand was like these boys, poor and with no place to live.

It seemed only a minute afterward that I was split away from them, Mum and Billy. It happened so quickly that I could barely tell how it happened in the first place.

With no warning, O'Toole jumped from my arms and sprung to the back of the wagon, barking furiously. The noise all around us was so tremendous that I could barely hear him, though he was only a few feet off in the back of the wagon. I turned and was startled by what I saw.

Like a shadow from a dark dream, a boy was crouched in the back of the wagon. He was thin, his clothing all in tatters, and I knew at once he was a **street urchin.** He was pawing frantically through our belongings, and before I could even move, I saw him snatch my leather box up in both hands. He tucked it under an arm and then looked up. Our eyes met.

The next minute, he had jumped down and back into the wild chaos of the street. O'Toole jumped from the wagon too, intent on chasing the boy and still barking furiously.

"O'Toole!" I screamed. On an impulse that had nothing to do with thinking ahead, I jumped to the street, too. I started off after O'Toole. Then I heard my brother scream my name and realized what I had done. I glanced back at the wagon and for a moment my feet were stilled, my mind torn. But the boy was disappearing into the mad crowd. Disappearing

with all the items that meant anything to me in this material world. And O'Toole was fast disappearing, too. I turned away from the wagon and ran.

The next moment a burning beam of timber crashed to the street behind me. It struck a man to the ground and instantly cut off my view of the street. Where, only seconds before, our wagon had been, there was now only a sea of human life and **debris,** outlined in flame. I could see nothing of Billy or Mum or the wagon at all. They had disappeared completely. I ran on after O'Toole and the boy.

I caught the boy in the block where the

Children like Armand often wandered the streets of Chicago. They had no homes and sometimes no parents. Sometimes they begged for—or even stole—food to survive.

28

courthouse stood, and I wrestled him to the ground. It was easy to do as he was so much frailer than I was. I grabbed my box from him and opened it quickly. I was relieved to see my watch. It read nearly 1:20. Hastily, I slipped the watch into my pocket and looked up. I had expected the boy to have dashed off into the night, but he was still standing there. And it was then that he hit me with a fist— in the chest and so hard it knocked the wind from me. But in the next second, his blow was forgotten, for suddenly there came an even more terrible sound. An unearthly roar. The ground all around us began to shudder as if a demon earthquake had been let loose. I looked up to see the courthouse bell tower above us wavering. It seemed even to scream as it went crashing, bell and all, from high above down into the center of the courthouse building, which itself was on fire.

The boy howled and dropped to the ground. I saw immediately that he had been struck on the back of his head by a falling brick. All around the **pandemonium** thickened. I saw several policemen leading prisoners away and realized they had probably come from the jail cells in the courthouse basement. I heard someone scream that the fire had jumped the river and was even

Some homeless children were "adopted" by adults, but actually they were just put to work in factories, sometimes working ten or twelve hours a day.

Firefighters did all they could to stop the blaze, but it was too big to control.

now eating up the finest homes in the northern division.

I wanted to run. But I didn't know which way to go to reach safety. Or even which way was west from where I stood. And then there was the boy. I knelt and tried shaking his shoulder. In a moment his eyelids fluttered. His eyes opened on me, and a wave of fear passed through them. He sat up quickly and rubbed the back of his head.

"Show me the way to my uncle's, and I'll be sure you get food and some clothing," I said to him. He looked at me suspiciously.

"But we've got to hurry!" I said, trying to sound urgent but calm at the same time so he wouldn't be alarmed. "Please? Where is the bridge that will take us over the river to the western division?"

The boy stood and brushed himself off. He moved slowly, as if maybe he were still dazed. O'Toole barked, the kind of bark that I recognized as a friendly greeting. His tail slapped back and forth. The slight hint of a smile curved the boy's mouth. I took a deep breath. My lungs hurt, as if they were burning inside my chest. We had to get out of there.

Armand, for that turned out to be the boy's name, listened closely as I told him my uncle's address and everything I knew about where he lived and how to get there. It wasn't

The Chicago Water Tower was dedicated at a big celebration in 1867 and was not badly damaged by the fire.

much, but Armand nodded.

"I know where," he said. "We go."

Armand was quick. He darted through the crowds, me beside him. O'Toole ran between us, growling and snapping at anything that seemed to threaten danger. As we passed, a man who looked mad stepped out from behind a **smoldering** wall and tried to grab one of us, but O'Toole drove him off.

All around us the city's destruction was in progress. We passed burning lumber yards, grain silos like pillars of fire. The sky was so bright with glaring, orange light that it was as easy to see as if it were daytime. But what we saw were only nightmare scenes. I followed Armand down an alleyway and suddenly we

Many big mansions in the Old Settlers neighborhood were destroyed by the fire. These homes belonged to wealthy families such as the Rumseys and the Odgens.

As the city burned, many people walked through Potters Field on their way to Lincoln Park.

were descending into a stifling tunnel. The Washington Street tunnel, he told me. Others were down there as well. It was so dark in the tunnel that their forms were only shadows, and I imagined them to be **ogres** as they fled in all directions.

As we came out of the tunnel, I immediately felt more coolness in the air. But the scenes of terror were no less. We hurried north and came to the Randolph Street Bridge. It was clogged with people and horses and wagons. A part of the railing had been broken away and I saw someone dive, or perhaps fall, into the oil-slick water of the Chicago River. Even the river was burning, because of the oil spills. The screaming was unending and I felt a sudden strange sickness. I was pushed violently by someone trying to get past us. Then a wagon rumbled behind me. I felt my body slam into a wooden wheel and felt myself being flung through the air. I thought I heard Armand shout my name as I landed with a thud and a crack. Then there was darkness. And silence.

Many of the poor people in Chicago suffered the most from the fire. They lost their homes and their businesses. And they didn't have insurance or other family members to give them shelter.

———

When I came to, I had no idea how much time had passed. Everything around me seemed much quieter now. I felt a calmness that hadn't been there before. Armand was squatting and staring at me steadily. O'Toole

The Randolph Street Bridge was jammed with people trying to flee the city.

Even after the fire, the air in Chicago remained hot for days. Some businessmen reported opening safes and having their important documents burst into flame when they came in contact with the scorching air.

The Great Fire was front-page news throughout the country and the world.

was whining and wagging his tail furiously. I tried to smile. Armand stood and turned, looking all around him. Then he began to walk. I got up and followed him, O'Toole close beside me.

Armand seemed to know his way. His every step was sure and determined, and I followed along, letting him take the lead. He caught us a ride on a wagon going in the direction of my uncle's, and we were soon in the right neighborhood.

As we stepped down from the wagon, a cold drizzle was beginning to fall. Death to the fire, I thought. It was dark and quiet in this neighborhood, far from burning embers and the cries of desperate human beings. I knew exactly where we were. We stood now in front of my uncle's home. I could see all the windows filled with light, and it appeared calm and cheery inside. I looked over at Armand.

He looked hesitant, as if he weren't sure about going inside. Then he dug in his pocket, and I watched as he pulled out my grandfather's pocket watch. I looked down and saw that the time was 11:11. Then I realized it must be Monday night already. Nearly twenty-four hours had passed since I'd first woken to fire. And now here we were, safe. I didn't mind that Armand was holding my watch. While we were going through the tunnel, he had told me he was an orphan and described his rough life alone on the streets. He was a brother to me now, and he had probably never had a thing as nice as that watch in his entire life. I felt glad he was looking after it.

I climbed the steps to my uncle's front door. Armand stood a moment on the wooden sidewalk, as if gathering his courage. Then he came up the steps, too. We knocked.

Inside we were met by all. Everyone was safe. My parents and both of my brothers. Other relatives and friends were there who had escaped, too. Armand spoke quietly to my family. I watched as there came wild and sudden tears. Armand held out the pocket watch to Papa, and I saw Mum slump to her chair, beating her fists against her knees and crying furiously. Then suddenly she embraced Armand as if he were her own

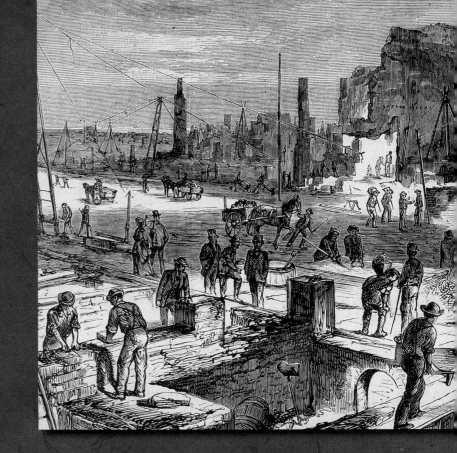

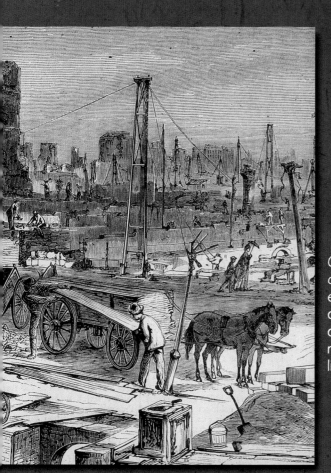

Once the rain fell and the fire finally ended, the people of Chicago took on the task of rebuilding their lives.

son. I knew they would take him in as family as easily as I had.

A deep sigh of peace came up out of me. My lungs didn't hurt anymore. That sigh came from so deep it was like a soft wind rushing through the room. Everyone looked up, as if they had heard something.

Brian and I nodded solemnly to one another as we looked down upon our relatives from a place up near the ceiling. It would be a comfort to them to be gathered there all together. Our loving family. Good people. Strong.

"They can sense us with them," Brian said.

"Yes," I agreed. "And Armand will fill the hole."

THE HISTORY OF
THE GREAT CHICAGO FIRE

Liam's family emigrated from Dublin, Ireland, to Chicago, Illinois, sometime during the 1860s and 1870s. They, like thousands of other starving immigrants, had come to America after a four-year **blight** in Ireland had wiped out the country's entire potato crop. They settled in large cities such as New York, Boston, San Francisco, and Chicago. In Chicago, families crowded into small wooden cottages on the Near West Side within a few blocks of one another.

In 1871, Chicago was the fourth largest city in the United States, and it was an industrial giant. The city had become the world's busiest rail center. The railroads brought cattle from the

West to fill Chicago's stockyards, creating grain, livestock, and lumber markets for the city. Most of the city had been built with wood. There were 57 miles (92 kilometers) of wood-paved streets and bridges, 561 miles (903 km) of wooden sidewalks, and thousands of wooden houses.

At the time of the Great Chicago Fire, the city was experiencing a dry season. Barely 1.5 inches (3.8 centimeters) of rain had fallen in the three months prior to October 8, 1871. When the fire began around 9 P.M. in or near Patrick O'Leary's barn on the Near West Side, it spread rapidly. The fire burned for 24 hours until a light rain put it out, revealing a burned area 4 miles (6.4 km) long and 3/4 of a mile (1.2 km) wide. At least three hundred people lost their lives in the fire and a hundred thousand lost their homes. The city lost $200 million in property.

Chicago began to rebuild immediately, using stricter building codes and better fire-proofing. It attracted many of the nation's finest architects. In a few short years, businesses like the one Liam's family owned were operating once again, and Chicago regained its title as one of the world's great cities.

GLOSSARY

bedclothes sheets and blankets

blight a disease or injury to plants that results in death

calamity a disaster causing great pain or sorrow

commotion noisy confusion

debris fragments of rock and rubble

din a loud noise that continues for some time

disembodied having no body

dread great fear in the face of an upcoming event

eerie strange in a scary way

embers pieces of wood or coal still burning in the ashes of a fire

hypnotic holding the attention of someone

lulling calming

TIMELINE

1818 On December 3, Illinois becomes the twenty-first state.

1837 Chicago is named a city, and its population is 4,170.

1860 Chicago holds its first national political convention, which nominates Abraham Lincoln as a Republican candidate for president.

1861—65 During the Civil War, Camp Douglas in Chicago is opened for recruits.

memsmerized spellbound, in a trance

ogres ugly giants in fairy tales

ominously in a threatening or foreboding way

pandemonium wild uproar

pneumonia a viral disease that causes the lungs to become inflamed and often fill with liquid

premonition anticipation of something without having any practical reason to expect it

smoldering burning slowly and without flames

spectacle a dramatic scene

street urchin a child who is usually poor or homeless and earns a living by begging or stealing

thoroughfares main roads

1870 The number of Irish-born Illinois residents reaches 120,162.

1871 On October 8, the Great Chicago Fire begins; on October 10, with 100,000 people left homeless and $200 million worth of property destroyed, rain begins to fall and the fire ends.

1873 In June, Chicago hosts a jubilee to celebrate its economic and architectural recovery from the fire.

1885 The Home Insurance Building, erected at the northeast corner of Chicago's LaSalle and Adams Streets, is called the first skyscraper and consists of nine stories and a basement. The site is now occupied by the west portion of the Field building.

1893 Chicago hosts the Columbian Exposition, a world fair celebrating the 400-year anniversary of Christopher Columbus's arrival in America.

ACTIVITIES

(Writing Creatively)

Continue Liam's story. Elaborate on an event from his scrapbook or add your own entries to the beginning or end of his journal. You might write about Liam's relationship with his brothers prior to the fire or how their lives changed after it. You can also write your own short story of historical fiction based on the Great Chicago Fire of 1871 or about the treatment of Irish immigrants living in Chicago in the late 1800s.

CELEBRATING YOUR HERITAGE

(Discovering Family History)

Research your own family history. Find out if your family had any relatives living in the Chicago area at the time of the Great Chicago Fire. Ask family members to write down what they know about the people and events during this time period. How were your relatives involved directly or indirectly in the fire? Make copies of old drawings or drawings of keepsakes from this time period.

DOCUMENTING HISTORY

(Exploring Community History)

Find out how your city or town was affected by the Great Chicago Fire. Visit your library,

historical society, museum, or local Web site for links to the event. How did eyewitnesses

describe the event? What did newspapers report? When, where, why, and how did your

community take action? Who was involved? What was the result?

PRESERVING MEMORIES

(Crafting)

Make a scrapbook about family life at the time of the Great Chicago Fire. Imagine what

life was like for your family or for Liam's family. Fill the pages with descriptions of special

events, family stories, interviews with relatives, letters, and drawings of family treasures.

Add copies of newspaper clippings, photos, postcards, and historical records such as birth

certificates and immigration papers. Decorate the pages and the cover with family heir-

looms, Liam's pocket watch, or a map showing the journey your relatives, or Liam's parents,

took by ship from Ireland to New York City.

TO FIND OUT MORE

AT THE LIBRARY

Alcraft, Rob, and Louise Spilsbury. *Fire Disasters.*
Crystal Lake, Ill.: Heinemann Library, 2000.

Balcavage, Dynise. *The Great Chicago Fire.*
Broomall, Pa.: Chelsea House, 2001.

Murphy, Jim. *The Great Fire.*
New York: Scholastic, 1995.

Robinet, Harriette Gillem. *Children of the Fire.*
New York: Atheneum, 1991.

Stein, R. Conrad. *Chicago.*
Danbury, Conn.: Children's Press, 1997.

ON THE INTERNET

Chicago Public Library: 1871, The Great Chicago Fire
http://www.chipublib.org/004chicago/timeline/greatfire.html
For photographs and a discussion of the cause of the fire

The Great Chicago Fire and the Web of Memory
http://www.chicagohs.org/fire/index.html
An online exhibit created by the Chicago Historical
Society and Northwestern University

The Library of Congress: The Great Chicago Fire
http://www.americaslibrary.gov/pages/jb_1009_chicago_1.html
For a brief description of the Great Fire

ON THE ROAD

Chicago Historical Society
Clark Street at North Avenue
Chicago, IL 60614
312/642-4600
To learn more about Chicago history

Harold Washington Library Center
400 South State Street
Chicago, IL 60605
312/747-4999
To view the Chicago Collections exhibits

A B O U T   T H E   A U T H O R

Pamela Dell has worked as a writer in many different fields, but what she likes best is inventing characters and telling their stories. She has published fiction for both adults and kids, and in the last half of the 1990s helped found Purple Moon, an acclaimed interactive multimedia company that created CD-ROM games for girls. As writer and lead designer on Purple Moon's award-winning "Rockett" game series, Pamela created the character Rockett Movado and twenty-nine others, and wrote the scripts for each of the series' four episodic games. Purple Moon's Web site, which was based on these characters and their fictional world of Whistling Pines, went on to become one of the largest and most active online communities ever to exist on the Net. Pamela lives in Santa Monica, California, where her favorite fun is still writing fiction and creating cool interactive experiences.